Disney·PIXAR
FINDING DORY

A Day with Dory

Adapted by Catherine Baker

Nemo was keen to have some fun ...

... but his dad, Marlin, had too many rules. Nemo got fed up with them.

Play *near* home!

Just *one* snack after school!

Go to bed *on time*!

One day, Marlin had to go on a trip. He asked Dory to look after Nemo and his friend Sheldon after school.

Dory happily agreed.

Nemo told Sheldon the good news.

It was good, because Dory always forgot things.

"This means no rules!" shouted Sheldon.

The little fish could hardly wait for school to be over.

When Dory came to pick them up, Sheldon asked if they could play at the coral reef.

"Sounds like fun!" said Dory, happily.

So they went to the reef ...

... which was against Marlin's rules!

Playing hide-and-seek at the reef was lots of fun at first, but then ...

... Nemo woke up a grumpy moray eel.

As he was trying to get away, Nemo stung his fin on some coral.

Dory gave Sheldon and Nemo a yummy after-school snack – plankton pizzas!

But then she forgot, and also gave them seaweed sandwiches ...

... kelp cookies ...

... *and* seagrass smoothies!

They started to feel very full.

It was getting late. Nemo knew it was time to go home, but first he wanted to play some extra games. So they had a game with a clam.

Bruce the shark wanted to play Splash Tag.

Next it was time for Dodge-coral ...

... and then they had a game of Toss the Sea Disc.

After a while, Nemo started to feel very, very sleepy.

Nemo was so sleepy that he couldn't catch the sea disc. It made a big hole in Mrs Puffer's house! Oh no!

"Sorry, Mrs Puffer!" said Nemo. He felt bad.
"I think it's time to go home," he told Dory.

When they got home, Nemo wanted to go to bed, but Dory still wanted to play!

So Nemo told her that going to bed on time was an important rule.

"You will feel better in the morning," said Nemo. "Trust me!"

Just then, Marlin came home. He heard what Nemo said.

"You sound just like *me*!" he laughed.

"Daddy, I'm so glad you are home!" Nemo cried. "Perhaps rules are not so bad after all."

"Thanks for everything, Dory!" said Marlin.

"I had a great time," said Dory. "Or at least, I think I did!"